D1029366

The Adventures of BG

Lucky Enough to See the World Differently

Written by Joe Freeman

Illustrated by Lameek Wilson

The Adventures of BG
Lucky Enough to See the World Differently

Published in the United States by JAX Publications
www.jaxpublications.com
Printed in the United States

ISBN 978-0-9983657-8-7
Library of Congress
Number 2020909804

Dedication

First, I want to give all honor to my Lord and Savior, Jesus Christ.

This book is dedicated to my biggest supporter and the love of my life, Shawntae and my inspirations: Jaylon, Maitae, Jace, and my nephew TJ. I also want to thank past and present students for showing me the beauty in paying close attention to details, in a world filled with distractions. You all are the reason I strive daily to become a better husband, father, uncle, educator and man.

Praise for The Adventures of BG

Inclusivity is the key to relationships and interactions between people. It was very refreshing that BG and his friends were able to figure out that Truesdale did not have a disability   and that he had special abilities. This group of friends was triumphant! Very inspiring read.
~Phillip M. D'Amico
Middle School Principal

It is imperative to raise awareness about health disorders to remove the stigma associated with them. Many kids who are diagnosed with a disorder are bullied and isolated because to the uneducated, they are not normal. To prevent this, educating our children about an array of health disorders is vital. This book "The Adventures of BG", demonstrates the importance of health education for our children. Being knowledgeable of others' uniqueness will change the perceptions of health disorders, and potentially promote acceptance and respect for those who are different from their peers.
~Tierra Jones, RN

Joe Freeman's latest book highlights how children can work together to recognize the differences amongst us but celebrate the similarities. Indeed, it is these similarities that can help us to help each other and make this world a more tolerant and giving place. And this learning needs to start early on!

~Robert A. Saul, MD

Question from the author: Would you rather prepare your child for the world or prepare the world for your child?

It was the morning after Fall Break and the only thing everyone could think about was their field trip to Trash Mountain. Trash Mountain was home to one of the best amusement parks in the city called Everglades over Florida. The park contained more than 20 thrilling rides. But more importantly it was full of stories about kids entering its golden doors never to be heard from again.

Everyone agreed that this trip would be the best one yet and they couldn't wait to go on their next adventure. However, BG would be the firstto discuss what he had heard about the famous ride at the park called "Gator Bait". This ride would take you through what seemed like 2 miles of twisting and turning before bringing you face to face with 10 of the biggest alligators anyone had ever seen. Then just before one of the ferocious animals would take a bite out of you, the ride would twist and turn you between the predators' teeth before launching you to safety. But not before most of its fearless riders would lose a shoe or a hat to one of the hungry gators.

Leon was the first one to disagree with the stories. He said he would prove them all wrong by being the first one through the gates of the park.

Then Robby and Manuel (who were rocking back and forth) had to share their stories of how they heard that no student ever left the park the same as they had entered it.

But before Big L could add her two cents, a new kid passing by, came from the shadows saying that the scariest part of the park was not the rides or the animals. It was getting lost and having to spend the next five years of your life wandering through the park trying to find your way out.

Shocked, the Fabulous Five (a nickname given to them by Leon's mom, Mrs. Mary) could not believe that they had not noticed this new kid eavesdropping on their conversation the entire time. Just as the crew turned to focus their attention on this new kid, Robby asked him to introduce himself. He could not wait to speak; he said his name was Hunter but everyone called him Truesdale.

Truesdale began to tell the crew that he was sorry for interrupting the Fabulous Five but he wanted them to know what to expect when they reached Trash Mountain. Unlike most kids Truesdale had a couple of secrets, that were almost like super powers. One was that he was excellent at paying close attention to very small details.

However, before he could finish the crew started talking to each other again, like he wasn't even there. This is when Truesdale grabbed the straps of his backpack and started to walk off. He knew then that they were going to treat him just like all of the other kids and refuse to listen to him - because of his appearance.

Truesdale was just like most of the students at Lake Shore Middle. He wanted to be seen and heard by people, especially the ones he liked the most. But unlike most 8th graders he was rarely spoken to. Maybe it was because he wore a set of green cushy headphones every day that never seemed to be connected to anything. Most students figured he wore the head phones daily because he didn't want to be bothered by anyone. And when he worked up his nerve to speak, students would just pretend not to hear him just like today. So, he did what he always does and just walked off, with his head down.

All of the kids watched Truesdale walk away, before turning and starting to talk again. Everyone except Manuel, who still remembered how hard it was for him to communicate with new people. But he could also tell that there was something special about Truesdale, even if he couldn't prove it at the time.

The crew was not in science class more than five minutes before they were asked to make their way down to the buses parked in front of the school.

Students from both 7th and 8th grades entered the buses looking to see who would pair up with them — everyone except Robby, whose allergies caused him to miss the field trip. Truesdale was the first to find an empty seat hoping someone would sit with him. He made sure he wasn't too close to the back in case he had to get out in a hurry. His dreams were kind of answered when Mrs. Freeman, a social studies teacher flopped down in the seat next to him.

By the time the bus driver began to close the door every-one had found a seat buddy. BG was with Manuel, Leon was with some random kid and Big L was with this new kid, Ronnie.

Before the bus could pull out of the school parking lot the sounds of laughter and dialogue between 48 kids filled the bus. That's when BG noticed Mrs. Freeman trying to get Truesdale to remove his headphones. BG quickly nudged Manuel (who was starting to cover his ears), to get his attention so both could see what would happen next. Ronnie and Big L leaned in too, hoping to see how Truesdale would respond. No one had ever seen Truesdale without his headphones on. Sensing something big was about to happen Big L turned, signaled Leon to stop what he was doing and focus his attention on Truesdale. Truesdale, who had never been known to be a disrespectful student, turned toward Mrs. Freeman, so she could ask him a quick question. Truesdale hesitantly began to slowly reach for his headphones when a paper fight broke out in the middle of the bus and Mrs. Freeman's attention shifted to the unruly students.

When Mrs. Freeman finally returned to her seat Truesdale had closed his eyes and pretended to be asleep for the rest of the ride. Before long a kid from the back of the bus yelled out "WOW! Look at this Place! I can't believe we're here!" At that moment everyone turned and stared in amazement because Trash Mountain was even bigger than they could have ever imagined. Next to that mountain was the best amusement park in the state of Florida. Now all the kids on the bus were on their feet.

"Everglades Over Florida"
has added three new rides:

"The Tunde" (Trail of Tears)

"The Yardo" (Yards of Screams)

**"The Oucha" (Better known as
The Big O-No!)**

That's when they spotted the neon green sign:

"Everglades over Florida" has added three new rides, "The Tunde" (Trail of Tears), "The Yardo" (Yards of Screams), and "The Oucha" (Better known as the Big O-No!).

That bus and every bus as far back as a mile went crazy with excitement and cheers.

Mrs. Freeman and the other teachers asked every student to look to his or her right and left. They then said that there would be over 5,000 people at the park today and it would be up to them to stay with their group. Immediately, the students were divided into 8 groups of 6. Each group was called a unit. Each group had 6 members except for BG's crew. That's when Mrs. Freeman placed Truesdale and Ronnie in their group. Ronnie was a short muscular kid with huge forearms who was known as "arms" to everyone around the school, because of his arm wrestling abilities. The crew quickly gave their new group members the once over and started heading towards the gate before Mrs. Freeman stopped them and said everyone had to meet her back at the entrance by 3:00, which meant they would have 4 hours to explore.

Once inside, their senses were aroused by smells of freshly popped popcorn, candy apples and the sounds of screaming kids running from roller coaster to roller coaster. Mist machines filled with free lemonade on every corner making sure no one overheated, only added to the thrill of the park.

Manuel and Big L wanted to go to the "Yardo" but Leon was mesmerized by the "Big O". Instead of separating BG suggested that they take a vote to decide which ride they would try first. They took a vote but noticed that there were two votes still missing. So they turned to Ronnie, who was too busy arm wrestling strangers for stuffed animals to notice that a vote was being taken. That's when they shifted their attention to Truesdale who seemed to have his eyes on the entrance of the park for some strange reason.

They had only been in the park for 10 minutes and Truesdale was already thinking about how he could get back to the bus. Without a clear decision on which ride to try first, the group decided to walk in the direction of the closest ride.

After walking for no more than 100 yards they came to a fork in the road where they noticed a map stand on the corner and a sign that read turn right for ride "Big O" or keep straight to find "The Yardo." Leon felt like they should stop at the map stand before making a decision. But Manuel convinced him that it would be a waste of time to stop. All they had to do was go in the direction of the rides and they would find them all in no time. Everybody decided to go straight while Ronnie ran to catch up. But Truesdale seemed to fall farther behind looking left to right but he eventually began to slowly follow.

They walked for what seemed like miles, stopping here and there for an occasional snack that included pizza, pretzels, popsicles, cheddar cheese popcorn and free lemonade from the mist machines. The time was now 1:30 and BG was the first to notice that the rides seemed to be getting farther and farther away and the park was starting to become scarier with every turn. What was once a park filled with wonderful smells of food and sounds of kids laughing, now was replaced with an eerie silence and abandoned food trucks.

The crew knew they were lost and like so many times before Truesdale was the first to speak up but this time things were different. Before BG could interrupt Truesdale, Manuel addressed his friends asking them to stop talking and listen to what Truesdale had to say. At that moment Truesdale removed his headphones and began to tell them how he could get them to all of the rides and safely back to the bus. But they must all agree to two things. First, they must never allow their quick assessment and little understanding of a person get in the way of doing the right thing. Secondly, they must agree to trust him as he leads them on the adventure of a lifetime. Like Manuel, everyone knew their best chance of finding the rides and their way back to the bus was with Truesdale. As Truesdale (the fearless headphone free leader) led his unit through the maze of burnt popcorn, half eaten corn dogs and mustard stained food truck windows, he could see and hear the ride "Gator Bait," getting closer.

Every step they took toward the ride the louder the sounds became! Truesdale could no longer tell which direction to go as the sounds began to consume him. He began to sweat and tremble uncontrollably. Truesdale was beginning to unravel. Suddenly, Truesdale dropped down on one knee seemingly paralyzed with pain as he began to hum and rock.

That's when Manuel looked closely at Truesdale. He noticed that he had never placed his headphones back over his ears. Big L noticing it too jumped right into action, sliding both headphones back over Truesdale's ears. Everyone expected Truesdale to immediately jump back to his feet; but he didn't. It took him at least 10 minutes to stop rocking from side to side and attempt to stand.

Leon was the first to ask Truesdale how the loud sounds made him feel. Truesdale quickly responded with, "imagine someone screaming in your ears with a blow horn over and over again. It could cause you to blank out and that's why I wear my headphones everywhere I go." They thanked him for being so honest and asked if he felt strong enough to lead them on. Truesdale slowly nodded as they began their journey again in search of all the amazing roller coasters. As he guided his friends, Truesdale explained that he has a spectrum disorder called Autism. Truesdale told the crew that Autism causes him to be very sensitive to sound, which is why he wears his headphones to school every day. However, he stated that Autism may look different for other kids. "Autism can affect kids differently; some can be very sensitive to smells, or light, or taste, or noise, and even touch. You will even have some kids that will talk to you but never look directly at you or not speak to you at all."

Manuel then tells the crew that a kid with autism might have trouble speaking, learning the meaning of words, making friends or fitting in. Dealing with changes (like trying new foods, having a substitute teacher, or having toys moved from their normal places) might affect others. Sometimes they unravel in crowds. Some rock back and forth when they are trying to express themselves. But not to worry you can't catch Autism like a common cold.

However everything about Autism is not negative. Autistic children often possess many positive traits. They are honest and rarely lie. They pay close attention to details. They have terrific memories. Some excel in various subjects such as math or science. Some can become great musicians.

They followed Truesdale through a maze of tall statues of wild animals when they noticed a strong smell of rotten food coming from behind the last abandoned food truck. There it was - the ride of their dreams - "The Great Gator Bait." It was much bigger than it appeared from the bus! Everyone cheered at once. Truesdale had done it! He was able to lead them out of harm's way and deliver them to the part of the park where dreams were made! BG was the first to strap himself on the ride, followed by the rest of the unit. They had the ride of their lives ducking and dodging some of the biggest and greediest alligators they had ever seen. Every turn seemed to have them second guessing their decision to get on the ride. Finally, Leon had had enough and wanted Truesdale to guide them to the next phase of rides. So before anyone could change his or her mind, they were off to their next adventure.

The next ride on Leon's list had to be "The Yardo" also known as Yards of Screams. But before they could have their fun screaming for their lives, they had to go through "The Palace of Lights", which was filled with over a million of the brightest, blinking, buzzing lights found in the country. Truesdale began to lead all five of his friends through this forest of lights appearing not to be affected at all by the intense shine. But before they could clear the wonderland of lights Truesdale noticed that Manuel was beginning to act strange, as if he was blind. Big L called out to him but he refused to take another step. Then he began to scream with pain as he used his hands to cover eyes, then his ears. No one understood what was happening but Truesdale. So he kneeled reaching out his hands in a gesture asking Manuel to trust him as he offered to guide him out of this place.

"Trust me, I understand what you are going through," said Truesdale as he began to place Manuel's hand on his shoulder. Manuel's pain almost seemed to go away at the sound of Truesdale's voice. But he kept his eyes closed and allowed Truesdale to be his guide. Truesdale began to guide Manuel in the direction of the strong aroma of food. When they cleared the lights Truesdale told Manuel it was safe for him to open his eyes. They all thanked Truesdale again for the quick actions he took to get Manuel away from the bright lights. Manuel began to tell his friends how the bright lights made his ears and his head ache with pain and his vision to become cloudy.

"I think we have had enough adventure for the day," said Leon, "besides it 2:30 and Mrs. Freeman wanted us back by 3:00." " Truesdale do you think you could guide us back to the bus," said BG in his softest voice. The group erupted in laughter - Truesdale being the loudest.

In a matter hours the unit had made a bond that could never be broken. They had learned more about each other in those few hours, than most would ever know about them.

Truesdale started off and 3 rights later they were staring at the entrance to Everglades over Florida Amusement Park sign again.

The crew had never made it to "The Trail of Tears," but they had cried enough that day and were happy to see Mrs. Freeman's face.

The kids left as individuals with their own personal concerns and returned as a unit that understood that not everyone reacts to situations the same way. But with patience and tolerance they learned to "never judge a book by its cover" and to treat everyone equally.

Discussion Questions

1. Could this story be true? Why or why not?

2. What words would you use to describe the main character?

3. How is the problem solved? (What is the solution?)

4. What is the scariest, funniest, saddest, or most interesting part of the story? Read it aloud.

5. Compare and Contrast people you may know, who are like the characters in this story? How are they the same? How are the different?

6. Why do you think the author chose the title for this story? How does it relate to the story?

7. Who is telling this story? Is there a narrator?

8. Describe how you think the main character feels in the beginning of the story. Describe the main character's feelings at the end of the story.

9. If you could have a conversation with one of the characters in the story, which character would you choose and what would you talk about?

10. What changes would you make to the story?

Kid Friendly Definitions

Autism Spectrum Disorder:

(say: AW-tiz-um) spectrum disorder is a difference in the way a kid's brain develops. Kids with autism may have trouble understanding the world around them. Other traits are:
Verbal expression problems
Learning the meaning of words
 Making friends or fitting in
Dealing with change/transition
Sensitivity to loud noises, bright lights, touching, tasting, and smelling

eavesdropping: the act of secretly listening

judge a book by its cover:
 one shouldn't prejudge the worth or value of someone or something by **its** outward appearance alone

meltdown: a breakdown of self-control

tolerance: willingness to accept behavior and beliefs that are different from your own

Meet the Author

Joe Freeman is a writer, father, and teacher. He is also a very adventuresome amateur explorer (though he has never actually knowingly discovered anything). Joe Freeman lives on the Eastside of Atlanta, Georgia, with his inquisitive therapist wife. He has three kids, one too cool for school (college student son), one seven year old overly athletic son and another very hands-on daughter.

This is the third book in **The Adventures of BG** series.

Meet the Illustrator

Lameek Wilson is a visual and graphic artist. He resides in Atlanta, GA.
He has received numerous awards for his artwork including the Fifth Congressional District of Georgia High School Art Contest sponsored by Congressman John Lewis and the Invitational Art Education Fair Award. He has also illustrated several books.